For my favourite creatures,
Leon, Juno and Rich – C.F.

I dedicate this book to Tegu, who
helped me to go beyond my limits
– L.G.

First published in Great Britain 2022 by Farshore
An imprint of HarperCollins*Publishers*
1 London Bridge Street, London SE1 9GF

www.farshore.co.uk

HarperCollins*Publishers*
1st Floor, Watermarque Building, Ringsend Road
Dublin 4, Ireland

Text copyright © Ciara Flood 2022
Illustrations copyright © Lucia Gaggiotti 2022
Ciara Flood and Lucia Gaggiotti have asserted their moral rights.

ISBN 978 0 7555 0147 2
Printed in the UK by Pureprint a CarbonNeutral® company
001

A CIP catalogue record for this title is available from the British Library.

Farshore takes its responsibility to the planet and its inhabitants very
seriously. We aim to use papers from well-managed forests
run by responsible suppliers.

WRONG!

Ciara Flood
Lucia Gaggiotti

Farshore

Deep in the jungle the animals had made a new swing.

"It's my go next," said Orangutan.

"And then me," said Slow Loris.

It was Hog.

He barged his way to the
front and grabbed the swing.

"You're **supposed** to wait your turn," Orangutan told him.

"I NEVER WAIT!" yelled Hog. "Move it or lose it, spaghetti arms."

Hog swung **higher** and **faster** until . . .

CRASH!

"What a **RUBBISH** swing!" Hog snorted.

And he looked around for something else to do.

"Hey, bushy brows, what do you call **this?**"

"It's my den," said Bear.

"**WRONG!**" yelled Hog.

"It's a pile of sticks."

And he kicked it down.

"You can't just go around breaking things!" gasped Bear.

"WHO'S GOING TO STOP ME?" laughed Hog.

"HAHAHAHA!"

All that running had made Hog thirsty.
"Oi, spiky heads! What are you drinking?"

"Coconut milk,"
said the porcupines.
"Would you like some?"

Hog slurped down every last drop.
"That was supposed to be for **all** of us!"
cried the porcupines.

"**WRONG!**"
shouted Hog.

"It was **ALL FOR ME!**
And it was **delicious!**"

Now he'd had a drink, Hog was feeling hungry.
"Hey, wrinkle bum! What fruit grows on that tree?"

"Those are figs," said Tortoise.
"And my bottom is not—"

"**WRONG!**"

bellowed Hog.
"Those are **my** figs."

But the figs were too high up for Hog to reach.

"FIGS! COME DOWN HERE AT ONCE!"

he roared.

The figs did not budge.
Hog snorted and stomped
and kicked the tree.

But still no figs fell down.

"What I need is something
to throw at them," said Hog.

"Don't even **think** about it,"
said Tortoise.

Just then,
some figs did fall down,
all on their own.

"Hooray! Figs for everyone!"
cheered the other animals.

"WRONG!"

yelled Hog.

"I'm taking **every single one** of them. See you later, furballs."

And he stomped and crashed away, eating the delicious, juicy figs as he went.

In fact, Hog was **SO** busy eating the delicious, juicy figs that he tripped.

The figs went flying through the air.

They rolled.

They bounced.

They stopped.

"Hey, stinky paws, give back those figs.

THEY ARE MINE!"

"My dear Hog, you are absolutely **right**.
I would not **dream** of eating your figs.

Come over here
and get them,
please do . . .

"They are all yours."

For the first time in a long while the jungle was quiet. The only sound was the wind.

It made the branches go **swish, swish.**

It made the leaves
go **rustle, rustle.**

It made the figs
go **plop, plop, plop.**

And there were enough
delicious, juicy figs . . .

for everyone.